Stop That Robot!

Written by Alison Sage
Illustrated by Gary Dunn

Collins

4

6

A story map

Ideas for guided reading

Learning objectives: use talk to organise, sequence and clarify thinking, ideas, feelings and events; extend vocabulary, exploring the meanings and sounds of new words; use language to imagine and recreate roles and experiences; link sounds to letters; read simple words by sounding out and blending the phonemes; retell narratives in the correct sequence

Curriculum links: Personal, Social and Emotional Development: Feelings

Interest words: stop, that, robot

Resources: toy robot; pictures of robots

Getting started

- Ask the children about their experiences with robots. Have they seen any? Do they know any stories about them? Have they seen them on television or in films?

- Look at the front cover and discuss what job this robot might be designed to do. Why does he have so many arms?

- Practise reading the title of the book together. Sound out the word *stop*. Help the children to make a sound for each letter. Blend the phonemes to say the word.

- Read the word *that* together. How many sounds can the children hear? Identify that there isn't always a sound for each letter.

- Read the question on the back cover together. Discuss what the robot is doing and predict what might happen in this story.

Reading and responding

- Walk through the book together, identifying what is happening in each picture. Question the children to support their decoding of the pictures, e.g. p2: *Why is the child looking so sad? What is Mum saying?*

- Help the children to recount the story in brief detail.

- Return to pp2-3. Ask the children to look very carefully at each picture and to describe what is happening.